Coyote
and the
Sky

Author's Note

Coyote and the Sky

is a Tamaya Pueblo

creation story about the

Animal People's journey

to the Fourth World.

Text ©2006 by Shkeme Garcia

Illustrations ©2006 by Victoria Pringle

20 19 18 17 16 15   7 8 9 10 11 12

LIBRARY OF CONGRESS CATALOGING-IN-PUBLICATION DATA

Garcia, Emmett Shkeme, 1969–

Coyote and the sky : how the sun, moon, and stars began /
Emmett "Shkeme" Garcia ; illustrated by Victoria Pringle.

p. cm.

ISBN-13: 978-0-8263-3730-6 (cloth : alk. paper)

ISBN-10: 0-8263-3730-9 (cloth : alk. paper)

1. Indian mythology—North America—Juvenile literature.
2. Creation—Mythology—Juvenile literature.
I. Pringle, Victoria, 1985– , ill. II. Title.

E98.R3.G36 2006

398.2089'974—dc22

2006008936

Manufactured in China in September 2015
by Toppan Leefung Printing Limited

Design and composition by Melissa Tandysh

Coyote and the Sky
How the Sun, Moon, and Stars Began

Story by Emmett "Shkeme" Garcia

Illustrations by Victoria Pringle

UNIVERSITY OF NEW MEXICO PRESS · ALBUQUERQUE

A long time ago,
the Animal People
decided to make a journey
up into our world,
the Fourth World.

Back then,
where we lived in the
underworld was called Shipap,
or the Third World.

The Animal People went to the
Leader of the Third World
and asked him for advice.

"What should we do when we
get to the Fourth World?"

And he gave them
great advice about
how they should all stay
together and watch out
for one another.

But there was one animal that Leader didn't allow
to join the other animals on their journey:

Coyote.

This was because he was always making mischief
or trying to trick someone out of food.

When everyone was ready, they
started to make their long journey.

The
Animal
People
began
to
climb
and
climb
up
into
the
Fourth
World.

When they arrived, it was very dark.

They could not see anything and kept bumping into one another.

They were scared.

"What should we do?"

they asked

each other.

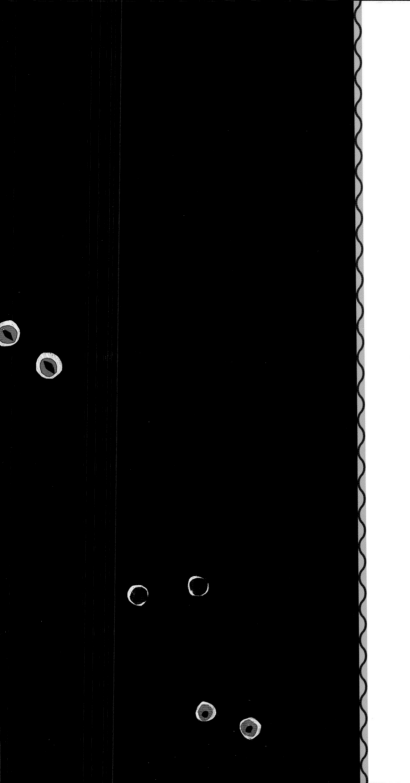

The Animal People huddled
into a close circle.

They decided to send
Squirrel and Rabbit back
down into the Third World
to ask Leader for more advice.

"There is no light in the Fourth World!

What should we do?" cried Rabbit.

Leader took some time to think about their problem.

Then he began to build a big fire, and while it was burning,

he began to make a yucca mat.

When he was done, the coals from the fire

were nice and hot and glowing.

Leader used a stick to put
all the coals onto the yucca mat
and tied it into a bundle.

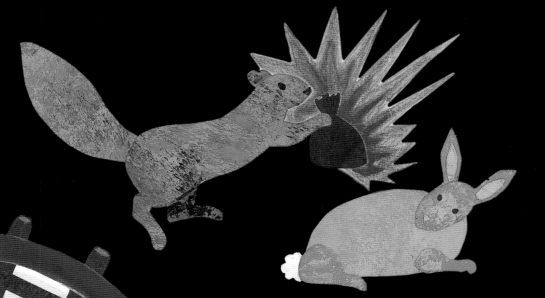

He told Squirrel and Rabbit to
run quickly with the bundle
up into the Fourth World.

When they reached the other Animal
People, they opened the yucca mat.

The Animal People grabbed each corner
of the mat and flung it into the heavens.

The glowing coals came together
into a big circle in the eastern sky
and became our sun.

At last,
there was light.
How beautiful it was!

But then the sun began
to move across the sky to the
west and soon disappeared,
and it was dark again.

"Now what should we do?"

The Animal People, once again, huddled into a small circle.

Again they decided to send Squirrel and Rabbit,

because they were the fastest,

down to the Third World to ask Leader what to do.

This time he made an even bigger fire, with bigger coals.

While it was burning he made another yucca mat.

When the mat was done and the coals from the fire were red and hot,

Leader took the coals and put them onto the mat.

Leader tied the mat
into an even larger bundle.

It was very heavy, and Rabbit
lifted the bundle with all her might
and ran up to the Fourth World
with Squirrel leading the way.

When they reached the Animal People,
they untied the bundle. They took
each corner of the mat and with
a great effort flung it into the heavens.

And this became our moon.

But still, it wasn't bright enough
and something was missing.

So Squirrel and Rabbit were sent down again
to the Third World to ask Leader what to do next.

This time he made an even bigger fire
and an even bigger mat!

All this time, little did they know

Coyote was hiding,

watching,

and listening.

When all was ready,

Leader wrapped the red hot coals in the mat

and told Rabbit to run as quickly as she could

back up to the Fourth World with Squirrel leading the way.

Rabbit could feel the heat from the coals,

and even to this day you can see

that Rabbit's eyes are pink from the heat.

But Rabbit was very brave.

She held the yucca mat out in front of her,

and all she could see was Squirrel's tail leading the way.

They did not know Coyote had come out
of hiding and was following them
up into
the
Fourth
World.

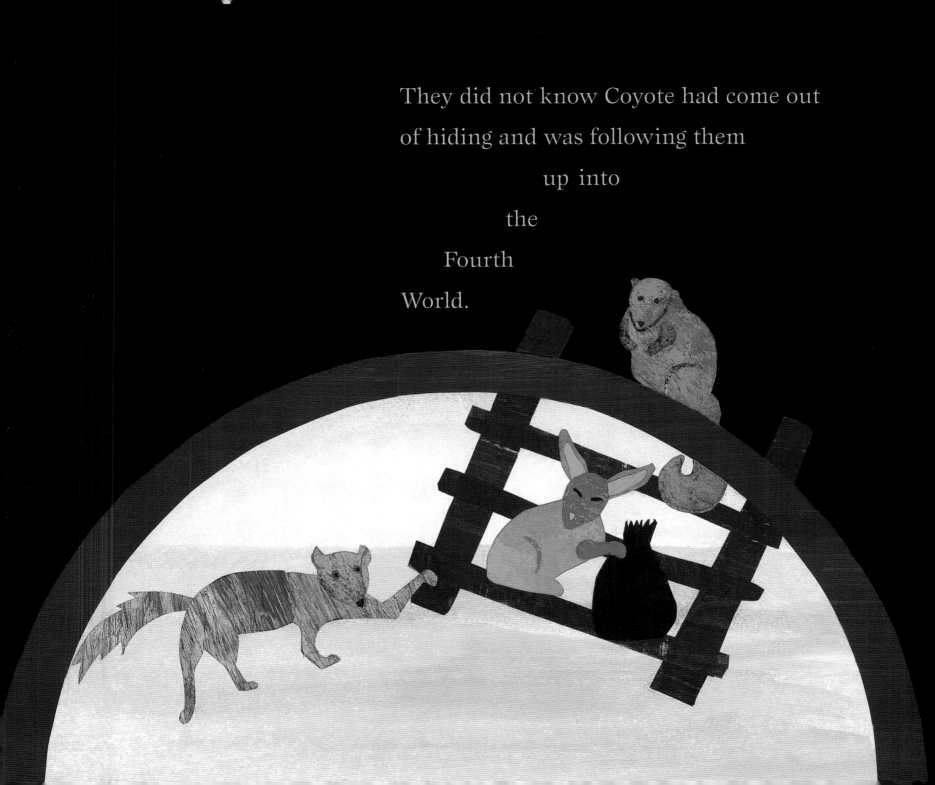

When they reached the other Animal People,
Coyote was very angry that he
had not been invited to come
to the Fourth World.

Coyote sulked behind a big rock
so that no one could see him.

When the Animal People opened
the big bundle, they asked Badger
to draw pictures of each animal on the
yucca mat with the red-hot coals.

Badger began to do so with a stick.

All this time Coyote was getting angrier and angrier.

Suddenly he jumped out from his hiding place

and grabbed one corner of the mat and flung it into the heavens!

These coals became our stars. And if you look closely at the stars today,

you can still see the outlines of the Animal People

that Badger drew on the yucca mat. These are our constellations.

In some places, the stars are in clusters, like in the Milky Way.

This is where Coyote messed up Badger's drawings.

Finally, Squirrel ran back to the Third World

to tell Leader what Coyote had done.

Leader decided to go up
to the Fourth World.

When he got to the Animal People, he
told Coyote that he had been bad and
must leave the Fourth World.

Leader put Coyote in a yucca mat and
threw him up among the stars
in the southeast corner of the sky.

He sent Squirrel into the northwest
corner of the sky to watch out for the
future of all the Animal People.
Today, this constellation
is known as the Big Dipper.

This is how the Sun,
Moon, and Stars
came to be.